Unforgiven

Colin Anderson

Ukiyoto Publishing

All global publishing rights are held by

Ukiyoto Publishing
Published in 2022

Content Copyright © Colin Anderson
ISBN 9789360168155

Dedication

To my beautiful wife Hannah, who is always my inspiration, and to kira for being an awesome friend. And to my mother Iin law Kim, who's put up with my constant re writes

Contents

Part 1: Betrayal...

"It is a wet and windy Friday afternoon in a busy well known rural town. A slumped figure drenched, trudges wearily home after finishing his shift for the day. We watch as he makes his way up a long steep hill towards a shared flat with his partner. He begrudgingly walks up two cold uninviting stone flights of stairs. He wearily turns the key and hears his partners voice on the phone. He enters the living room after closing the front door to give her a hug, but she pulls away and rudely indicates she's still on the call, and then she abruptly hangs up.

Woman

(Annoyed)

I was on an important phone call.

Man

I only wanted a hug baby.

Woman

I don't want you to touch me, Rob.

Robert Sanders

Why not!

Kirsty Watson

You repulse me.

Robert Sanders

(Defeated)

Oh... I always hug you when i come in from work!

Kirsty Watson

I don't want your fucking, shitty hugs. You'll have the weekend all to yourself. I'm going to my friends. You've changed, you never want to go anywhere.

Robert Sanders

(Annoyed)

I'm doing all the fucking shifts I can, I'm tired, plus your never fucking here anyway. You always complain that you have no money... quit fucking spending it then.

Kirsty Watson

(Fake Crying)

How dare you! How FUCKING dare you. Its all about money, with you.

Robert Sanders

No, it's you... I'm so sick and fucking tired of the same old shit... Money this, money that!

Kirsty Watson

Your not the same person I met that night. I can't even joke, or have a laugh with you anymore. You don't even do housework. Even on your days off.

Robert Sanders

I'm not spending my time off fucking cleaning. I'm tired from work. Its YOU that never cleans, you lazy bitch.

Kirsty's phone rings again and she walks out the room, still fake crying. Robert takes off his work clothes and slumps tiredly onto the couch only in his boxers. He stares into space, thoughts racing through his head. All he hears is the front door slam shut.

Robert Sanders

(To Himself)

Good fucking riddance...

He looks out the large bay window, as the sun begins to fade into the creeping night sky. He watches as people dressed in going out clothes laughing and drinking. He knows he has to go back to work tomorrow. His eyes begin to glaze with tears. He can't hold back his sadness and sobs

Robert Sanders

(To Himself)

I fucking hate this. Folk going out, and I'm stuck in this shitty flat... alone

He stops sobbing and wearily gets up turning everything off, and checking the door is locked as he makes his way to bed. He's about to enter the bedroom they share but stops himself. He sighs reluctantly as he makes his way into the spare room. He stares at the lowly single bed defeated and slowly lays down and listens to the revellers outside as he eventually falls asleep...

==

We hear the constant loud beeping from Roberts phone. He groans and through one sleepy eye and sees its **4:55am** as he grumpily wakes up and in his zombie- like state unconsciously gets out of bed and dressed for his shift which he knows starts soon. After a few short moments we watch as Robert walks to a well known retailer. He waits impatiently for whoever is opening up. After seems what feels like an eternity a small silver car pulls up. He smiles weakly as the person exits her car.

Woman

Morning Rob.

Robert Sanders

Morning Alexis, how's you this fine morning.

Alexis Thompson

Not too bad, you ready?

Robert Sanders

(Smiles Weakly)

Ready as I'll ever be.

Alexis opens the shutters, they grind stubbornly into life. Next she unlocks the automatic doors and both of them enter as the lights flicker on as Alexis disarms the alarm system. Moments seem to pass quickly as Rob is now behind the counter, ready to serve. We watch as customers come and go. Robs shift goes quickly. He is glad its almost over. Two friends of Kirsty walk in laughing and giggling. One of them is tall and clearly overweight and the other is slim and short. They grab some drinks and make there way to the counter. They spot Rob, and there laughing stops as there expression changes. They look at him with disgust as Rob scans there drinks.

Robert Sanders

(Begrudgingly)

Is that everything for you?

Andrea Smith

(Scoffs)

Uh... yes, duh!

Lucy Evans

I see Kirsty went to Rebecca's, for the weekend!

Robert Sanders

(Plays Dumb)

How did you two know?

Andrea Smith

She uh, called us about you. You never take her out
for a drink, or a meal anymore. She's going off you....

Lucy Evans

Take the hint pal, she doesn't want to be with you
anymore.

Robert Sanders

I'm not discussing our personal life, here.

Andrea Smith

Whatever pal, you think what you want... We know
different...

They both scoff as they snatch there change from
Rob. He forces a smile as they leave. The other
member of staff comes to the counter and relieves
Rob. He breathes a sigh of relief. And nods goodbye
to Alexis, who in turn nods back. We follow as he
gets his coat and puts it on and walks out the store

We watch as Rob walks up the long lonely road
home. We see people in a nearby local pub laughing,

smoking and drinking. He quickly glances at them, but abruptly stops as he sees Kirsty laughing and drinking with her friends. He notices a random guy join the group. He leers over Kirsty and she doesn't react. He gropes her breast and she doesn't flinch. Rob storms over into the pub and drags the man's arm off Kirsty.

Rob Sanders

(Pissed)

Get your fucking filthy claws, off my fiancée you pervert!

Man

Come on man, I was only having a laugh.

Lucy Evans

Yeah Rob, chill. You don't own her. She can do what she wants.

Kirsty

(Visibly Annoyed)

Your ruining my night Rob, go home and do whatever. I don't fucking care.

Andrea Smith

Take the hint, your not fucking wanted.

Lucy Evans

Yeah, piss off Rob.

Robert Sanders

Is... that what you want babe?

Lucy Evans

Ugh! Your making me sick.

Andrea Smith

Yeah she does, fuck off... now!

Robert Sanders

I wasn't asking for your opinion, bitch... Well?

Kirsty Watson

Go... just go... I'll see you when I get home.

Lucy and Andrea shoo Rob away. He walks away, his heart is breaking as he watches his so called fiancée and her friends carry on laughing and drinking as if he doesn't exist. Kirsty grabs the man's arm back round her. He smiles and again grabs her breast. Rob stands there dumbfounded, his eyes fill with tears. Pain etched on his face, he walks out the pub. He passes the window and stares at them. They don't even acknowledge him. He walks up the steep hill and eventually makes it home. He bumps into one of his friends.

Robert Sanders

Hey bud, how's you?

Mike Davies

Not too shabby, you off out tonight?

Robert Sanders

I might.... yeah fuck it. Two can play that game. Meet you in the pub in half an hour. I'm off for two weeks anyway , I didn't even know I had holidays... till today.

Mike Davies

Awesome, about time you came out with the boys. I'll make a few calls and you get yourself dressed.

Rob smiles genuinely and rushes off home excitedly. We follow Mike to the pub. He walks in and notices Kirsty and her friends but who just simply ignore him, as he proceeds to the bar and orders two lagers.

A few moments later Rob enters in a impressive grey suit, black loafers and a blue tie. A random group of ladies sniff his aftershave as he walks by and one of them has instantly fell in love. He strides up to Mike and pats him on the shoulder and he turns round. Mike is stunned.

Mike Davies

Woah, check you out dressed to the nines.

Robert Sanders

Not often I do.

Mike Davies

True, drink up. You deserve it.

Robert Sanders

And well overdue.

They both laugh out loud. Andrea taps Rob on the shoulder and he turns round.

Robert Sanders

What?

Andrea Smith

I thought I told....

Robert Sanders

Fuck off Andrea I'm enjoying my night.

Andrea

She doesn't want you here. Go home.

Mike Davies

Listen up miss yoyo knickers, he's out with me and
the boys, so piss off.

Robert Sanders

Yeah, run along little sheep... Baaaa.

Andrea storms off and quickly returns with Lucy and
Kirsty.

Kirsty Watson

You were told to go h....

Robert Sanders

You don't control who I see or go.

Lucy Evans

This is our spot, go find another pub.

Mike Davies

You don't own the pub, now trot on little horseys

Robert Sanders

Piss off, and leave us alone.

They are about to speak, but are cut off by a deep booming voice behind them. Mike and Rob smile as the girls turn around to see a 6ft 8 giant towering over them and a group of lads.

Man

Like they said, piss off.

They quickly scuttle away and the group all laugh. They and the tall man give Mike and Rob bear hugs.

Mike Davies

Easy boys! How are you Harry? Keeping your nose clean?

Harry Lewis

Trying micky boy, trying. Bobby boy, you doing ok?

Robert Sanders

Getting there H, getting there.

Mike Davies

What's all this mushy shit? Let's... get...
WANKERED.

They all cheer happily as the night goes on. They get drunker as every hour passes. The group of lads start to leave one by one, giving a little salute as they do. Harry eventually stumbles out and drunkenly salutes and carries on exiting the pub, as Mike and Rob laugh. Mike is the next to stumble out the pub and salutes Rob as he leaves. Rob looks at his watch and it reads **11:59pm.** Things start to go hazy , then turn black...

===============================

Part 2: Downward Spiral

The blackness begins to fade. Rob lays in a deep sleep in his now dishevelled suit. His tie is gone and his top button on his shirt is undone. He is clearly passed out drunk on an unfamiliar couch. He stirs momentarily and groggily groans as he awakens from his drunken stupor. His hangover rapidly waves over him. He temporarily tenderly shakes off the cobwebs from his foggy mind, to get his bearings. He quickly realises its not his flat. He hears clattering from the nearby kitchen. He unintentionally coughs and it grabs the occupants attention. A woman in a silk nightgown enters, it reveals the bra and thong beneath. She smiles seductively at him.

Woman

(Purrs)

Morning big boy!

Robert Sanders

(Hoarsely)

How... who...

Woman

It's me Chloe, from the pub!

Robert Sanders

I honestly don't remember much.

Chloe Davidson

You charmer. Oh, that wet patch in your boxers? You haven't pissed yourself, it's my pussy juice. Nice big cock, you have.

Robert Sanders

You... mean we... fucked?!

Chloe Davidson

(Giggles)

Oh yes we did, lover. Seven times actually. My, what stamina you have.

Rob rapidly sobers up. He looks at his phone to see he has 4 missed calls. He mutters "fuck" under his breath.

Robert Sanders

(Sighs Heavily)

Listen Chloe, I... uh... well... I have a fiancée.

Chloe Davidson

Oh her, yeah I know all about that cow! We went to the same high school. She'll use and abuse anyone, to get her way.

Chloe walks over and sits next to him and tenderly places her hand on his knee.

Robert Sanders

It's hard, living with someone who... literally hates your guts. I don't care if we made love, we...

Chloe Davidson

I know babe, I know. That's why from now on your my baby and I'll take care of you, don't you worry about money ok? . We can deal with that slut.. when the time comes.

She kiss his cheek lovingly as Rob gingerly gets to his feet, Chloe helps him and he smiles at her. She gives him a key and walks him out. She kisses him goodbye as he walks into the blinding sun. It makes him blink

for a few minutes. Then takes out his phone and dials.
Eventually Kirsty picks up.

Kirsty Watson

Where the fuck have you been? I've been calling four
times.

Robert Sanders

Look, you knew where I was. I crashed out at a mates
house.

Kirsty Watson

You mean some tarts house, no doubt.

Robert Sanders

Why does that matter? You had some random guy
feel your tit. Did you stop him? Besides... STOP
FUCKING TRYING TO CONTROL ME.

Kirsty Watson

DONT SHOUT AT ME DOWN THE PHONE,
CUNT!

Robert Sanders

(Inhales Calmly)

Besides, your at Rebecca's.

Kirsty Watson

I popped home for a clean pair of clothes. And you weren't here. You didn't do any washing. So, you can....

Robert Sanders

(Through clenched teeth)

Don't... you... fucking... dare. I am not doing shit. Here's a hint for you. Use... the... washing machine, you fat lazy bitch!

Before Kirsty can respond Rob hangs up and turns his phone off. He sees Mike and whistles for his attention. He jogs over to Rob and gestures for him to change. Chloe passes in her pimped out black with red trim Toyota. He stops and rolls down the tinted window. She wolf whistles at Rob and gestures to him to get In. Mike smiles cheekily and urges Rob on. He climbs in and Chloe hugs and kisses him. Unbeknownst to them, Lucy has spotted them. Mike desperately tries to call Rob...

Several hours later we see Chloe's car pull up outside the block of flats. Rob exits and Chloe kisses and hugs him. He is dressed in comfortable clothes. Kirsty is angrily waiting for him. His warm smile instantly disappears.

Kirsty Watson

So this is how it is! Hanging around with the village bike?

Robert Sanders

(Angrily)

Don't you fucking talk to her, like that. She actually cares about me... unlike some people I could mention.

Kirsty Watson

I care about you. I buy you nice things.

Robert Sanders

(Sarcastically)

Yeah, when you feel like it.

Chloe turns off the engine, and exits her car and shuts the door. She is dressed in jeans, sexy black top, boots and leather jacket and trendy sunglasses. She calmly walks straight up to Kirsty and slams her against the nearby wall, squeezing her neck. She just stares menacingly at her. Kirsty just stands there frozen in fear.

Chloe Davidson

Listen up bitch, he's my man now. And I'm going to treat him right, the way a partner should be treated. Not the way you do. Don't stand there and act like the perfect fiancée, because your not. Oh... I know all about last night... there's only one man who gets to feel my tits... My Robbie.

She lets Kirsty go and she slightly coughs for air while reflexively rubbing her throat.

Kirsty Watson

Your... your not having him... he's... mine. I... love him...

Chloe Davidson

(Laughs Sarcastically)

Listen to yourself. You don't love him, you never did. This started the moment he took a slightly lower paid job. That's when you started ghosting him. You mentally and physically drained him. To the point he gave up fighting.

Kirsty Watson

That's a lie Chloe, and you know it. It's not about money.

Chloe Davidson

That's bullshit Kirsty, and you know it. You wanted him to buy you everything, as soon as he got paid. He did that, happily for a while. You got pissed at him when he said no. The stress of his old job, sadly got the better of him. Did you comfort him? Tell him it was going to be ok, with this new job? Did you fuck!

Kirsty Watson

Your only using him, to get back at me. Only because you fancied him, back in high school. And you got jealous because I shagged him first.

Chloe Davidson

Listen to yourself, you deluded bitch! This isn't high school anymore. Get your head out your fat arse, and get into the real world.

Kirsty Watson

He's mine Chloe, and always be....

Robert Sanders

No Kirsty, I'm not yours to manipulate or to use as your personal cash machine. Its over... I can't do this anymore.

Kirsty Watson

(Fake Sobbing)

C'mon baby.... don't say that. I love you.

Robert Sanders

No... you didn't Kirsty! You only wanted me for my money. My old job, did get too much for me. I wanted a change, for my own health. You snapped at me when I told you.

Kirsty Watson

You caught me off guard baby, that's all. C'mon... let's go in and talk about it, as a couple.

Robert Sanders

You mean belittle me? Twisting the truth, so I come out as the bad guy! No... I'm done, it's done... We're done!

Rob removes the engagement ring off his finger and places it in Kirsty's hand. He looks at her one final time, gives her a friendly hug and smiles. He then turns and walks away arm in arm with Chloe. She watches as they both share a laugh as they climb into the car and it drives off Her fake sobbing quickly turns into real tears of sadness, then rapidly to rage and pain. Her fists clench tightly and her body shakes with anger.

Kirsty Watson

(Through clenched teeth)

Oh, we're not done Robert.... not by a long shot....

Part 3: Unsweet Revenge

Kirsty is sitting in Andrea's living room, bawling her eyes out. Rebecca is also there comforting her. Lucy is pacing up and down visibly angry.

Kirsty Watson

Why? Just.... why!

Lucy Evans

Fucking cunt, I'll kill him!

Andrea Smith

You gave him six years of your life, how does he repay you? By shagging another bird.

Kirsty Watson

I've... I've lost the man I love... forever. He even gave me back the ring I got him.

Lucy Evans

Bastard, I'll ring his fucking scrawny neck.

Andrea Smith

(Smiles Cunningly)

You still got his bank details, or his card?

Kirsty Watson

No, he'll have changed it by now. He's not dumb. Also he has extra security on his account, just as a precaution.

Lucy Evans

Fuck! Clever bastard.

Andrea Smith

He's not so stupid , I'll give him that.

Kirsty Watson

(Sighs Defeated)

Just, just leave it... its done and dusted now. No chance of getting him back now.

Lucy Evans

I have an... idea! If we can't hurt his wallet, we'll hurt something else. And I'm not talking about his job.

We drift backwards then spin round to see Chloe and Rob in a fancy Italian restaurant sitting at a table, with a little fake candle laughing and eating.

Chloe Davidson

You didn't have to do this babe. I would've...

Robert Sanders

You've let me move in, and you won't let me pay for anything. So this is my way, of saying thank you.

Chloe Davidson

(Smiles Sweetly)

Aww, your just so adorable baby...

Robert Sanders

(Blushes)

Stop....

Chloe Davidson

Its true. Even in high school. You... remember what I....

Robert Sanders

I do bubba, that's why I did everything to make you smile. Even though you were a snoot.

Chloe Davidson

(Fake Shocked)

Rude! Just Rude.

They both burst out laughing, unbeknownst to them there being watched. Two muscular figures watch them from a nearby alley way and mentally note there every move. Moments later we see them leave the restaurant and walk to the nearby pub. Chloe heads inside as Rob lights up a cigarette. He is approached by the two men. Rob glances curiously at them briefly. Suddenly they rush him and begin to beat him up. Rob puts up a good fight as Chloe and the bouncers rush out to the commotion. The two thugs are on the ground severely beaten up. They quickly scuttle to there feet and run off.

Rob is breathing hard, bloodied and bruised. He fixes his clothes and shouts after them.

Robert Sanders

YEAH YOU BETTER RUN. THATS YOU GET FOR MESSING WITH A ROYAL MARINE BITCH!

Chloe Davidson

(Concerned)

What did they do to my baby! Are you.... no, don't answer that. Dumb question.

Robert Sanders

Nothing I can't handle. I had better fights with my C.O.

The bouncers check Rob over and nods he's ok. Chloe helps Rob as he limps and they make there way back to Chloe's flat. We see Lucy and Andrea across the road. Rob stops and stares at them coldly. Rage is in his eyes, but he keeps his cool. As if to say " I know you did this" The two girls feel uneasy as Robs icy cold glare sends shivers up there spines, as they both run off. Chloe ushers him along shouting obscenities at the fleeing girls.

Later, we are back inside Chloe's flat. She is tending to robs cuts and bruises with Dettol. He winces slightly in pain. And looks at her and smiles. We see paper towels soaked in robs blood on a side table. He smiles at her, reassuring her he's fine.

Robert Sanders

Babe! I'm ok, my training will never leave me. I was in special ops, surprisingly to my superiors I quickly rose up the ranks. You probably noticed my full sleeve tattoo on my arm. Through my ripped shirt.

Chloe Davidson

I did baby, so... why did you really leave your old job? You can tell me... it's ok.

Robert Sanders

(Sighs Remorsefully)

One word, stress. Not because of the job itself... That.... fucking bitch! Constantly wanting money to spend on shit, we didn't even need... eventually it all came to end. I had to.... The definitely shit hit the fan when I cut her off...

Chloe Davidson

Let me guess, laying on the guilt. Making you out the bad guy. She's always been an manipulative cow. She always has, she'll never change.

A knocking is heard coming from the door. Rob musters all the strength to get up to answer it. He opens it to reveal Kirsty standing there in tears.

Rob inhales calmly to keep a cool head. Chloe sees her and instantly goes on the attack trying to get to Kirsty, but easily stops her and gives her the " I'll handle this look". Chloe calms and walks way while glaring menacingly at her. Rob closes the door gently as he just stares at Kirsty.

Robert Sanders

(Calmly)

You've got some fucking balls, to show up here...

Kirsty Watson

(Sad)

I...um.... heard what happened. And came to....

Robert Sanders

To what? See if your little scheme worked?

Your talking to an ex marine, Kirsty! What you'd think would happen? I'd just... stand by and let your thug cousins beat shit out of me?

Kirsty Watson

I had no idea, this would happen.

Robert Sanders

Don't fucking play dumb Kirsty, I know how you work... remember. Get this through your thick head, I **NEVER...** want to see you... again....**EVER!**

Rob opens the door and re-enters the flat, but stops.

Robert Sanders

Oh, one last thing... Sleep with one eye open....

He continues to enter and Chloe is seen giving her the finger and smiling as the door closes shut and is locked. Kirsty just stands there slowly realising her dreams are crashing down around her like broken glass. She sadly turns and scuffs her way out the flat, and up the same hill to an unwelcomely lonely dark flat...

Part 4: Plan Of Action...

Rob is bent over the counter at his work, staring blankly into space. He is roused from his daydreaming by Lucy standing there nervously with a meal deal. He gets to his feet and smiles, which puts her on edge. He scans her items, not taking his eyes off her.

Lucy Evans

(Nervously)

Hi... hi Rob. How's your day going?

Robert Sanders

(Eerily Calm)

Don't play nice Lucy, I know what you did. Oh yes, I know. But there was a flaw in your plan... don't... fuck... with a.... marine... bitch!

Lucy Evans

(Laughs Nervously)

Your so funny, I forgot how funny you were.

Rob Sanders

(Whispers)

Do you see me laughing bitch? This isn't a game. I know you were all in on it. Oh, there will be payback, trust me they'll be plenty of that... Have a nice day!

Rob smiles and it makes Lucy very uncomfortable. She turns and exits the store. She turns to look at Rob who eerily waves at her as she quickly walks on. A few minutes later Andrea enters the store, mentally scanning to see where Rob is. She temporarily breathes a sigh of relief as she heads to the counter. Rob smiles wickedly at her. She tries to pretend it doesn't bother her, but Rob knows different.

Andrea Smith

(Nervously)

Can I... have a pouch of tobacco, please.

Robert Sanders

(Sickly Sweet)

Oh of course madam, the usual?

Andrea Smith

Please...

Rob goes to the tobacco section behind the counter, and retrieves a pouch of tobacco and returns to Andrea.

Robert Sanders

There you are madam!

Andrea Smith

That's a nasty... scar you have there, Rob.

Robert Sanders

(Ironically)

Oh I wonder where I got that from....

Rob stares at Andrea smiling. She doesn't take her eyes off him as she takes her change and tobacco. And slowly slinks off.

Robert Sanders

(Eerily)

Have a nice day now.

Hours seem to fly by as we now are seen inside Rebecca's house. Lucy, Kirsty and Andrea are sitting discussing things

Lucy Evans

We shouldn't've done this.

Andrea Smith

He deserved this.

Kirsty Watson

How can I be so blind.

Lucy Evans

(Annoyed)

Oh and... thanks for the heads up Kirsty, you never mentioned he was an ex marine.

Rebecca Harris

(Shocked)

Didn't you see his tattoo? Oh you fucking stupid bitch! Now he'll be more dangerous, he won't stop until he gets who crossed him. Oh... fuck...

Kirsty Watson

What?!

Rebecca Harris

Do you know what regiment he was in?!

Lucy Evans

No, why?

Rebecca Harris

Special ops, you fucking dumb cunts! That's worse than being in the marines itself...

Andrea Smith

We're fucked!

Kirsty Watson

I'll just talk to him. Get him to back off.

Lucy Evans

(Angry)

Are you fucking kidding me Kirsty? He's a fucking ex marine you dozy cow. Once his skills kick in that's it. You might as well emigrate.

Kirsty

So what, I can still sweet talk him.

Rebecca Harris

He's a fucking ex marine Kirsty. You can't just... sweet talk him. I agree with Lucy, he won't back down or stop... you've just signed your own death warrant.

Lucy Evans

I agree with Rebecca, he had that... certain look in his eye.

Rebecca Harris

That's his codename persona, kicking in.. "Dead Eye" and it wasn't given for his clay pidgeon shooting skills. He was a supreme marksman...

Rebecca's house phone rings. The girls are on tender hooks as Rebecca picks it up and puts it on loud speaker.

Rebecca Harris

Hel... hello?

Robert Sanders

(Coldly)

I know your there with your cohorts, Kirsty. Rebecca you don't have to worry, your not part of this. But please don't get involved.

Rebecca Harris

Gladly.

Kirsty Watson

(Nervously)

H... hi baby.

Robert Sanders

Don't... you can't sweet talk your way out of this. I might just pay you a... little visit... if that's what you want.

Lucy Evans

N.. no, please Rob! We're sorry ok?

Robert Sanders

Oh, we're way past that! Anything you want to add you two.

Andrea Smith & Lucy Evans

No.

Robert Sanders

Your learning. Now, I'll keep this brief... I will see you all... **REAL** soon.

The phone goes dead and we hear a dial tone. Rebecca puts the phone back down and shakes her head in disappointment.

Lucy Evans

You don't get off that easy, Rebecca. You're involved. You didn't stop this.

Rebecca Harris

(Laughs)

Much more entertaining I didn't. I knew all along he'd do this... that's why it's hilarious.

Kirsty Watson

I'll dob you in, if you don't...

Rebecca Harris

What? Just go along with it? He'll see right through you. It'll make him more angry, if you drag me into it.

Lucy Evans

I don't want to imagine what he'll do.

Andrea Smith

Me neither, we'll apologise... then he will see sense.

Rebecca Harris

What the fuck is wrong with you all? He's ex military you dumb fucks. He won't care for your shitty apologies. It will just antagonise him more...

Part 5: Unstoppable Force...

Rob is in the store back office. He is sitting waiting patiently for his manager, staring blankly into space. A few moments later, his manager enters and is surprised to see him. Rob smiles genuinely at David, he gets up and closes the door. And sits back down and faces him.

Robert Sanders

Listen... I have something to tell you.

David Ross

Sure Rob, you can tell me anything...

Robert Sanders

(Sighs Heavily)

You... you know I served in the military right?!

David Ross

Yeah, something tells me you weren't in the regular army.

Robert Sanders

Marines actually, special ops.

David Ross

Oh.... I see...

Robert Sanders

Somethings have... come up, and I have to... see to
them.

David Ross

I see, and these things are?....

Robert Sanders

I.... can't say.

David Ross

I understand Rob. You've been a real asset. I'm sad to
see you go...

Robert Sanders

Likewise Dave, you've been a brilliant boss. But I
can't work here no more, I don't want anything to
come back to you...

David Ross

I heard what had happened that night, say no more. You don't want me to get the cop's involved...

Robert Sanders

It be best not to, they'd be collateral. Nothing more... Well, all the best Dave

David Ross

You too Rob... Good hunting.

Robert smiles as he stands up and makes his way out the office. His six sense then takes over, knowing that David would be tempted. But knows deep down, he wouldn't jeopardise his own life. Rob heads straight to the toilet to change. Several moments later, we see him exit in black spy clothes, impressive and imitating armour and a black biker helmet on, the visor is only one way. And he turns on a voice distorter on his neck. He has weapons concealed on him, and his trademark black and red sniper rifle strapped to his back.

He sneaks out the open back door of the store and into the night. Luckily it's so dark you can't see him. He makes his way to a nearby lock up. There sits a modified Yamaha bike in black. Rob is clearly prepared for what he must do. He sees a bus pass by and clocks his first target. He quickly jumps on his bike and gives chase. All we can hear is a faint whistle from the engine. As he has heavily modified it, to not make any noise. And it has armour plating, and a reinforced windscreen.

He keeps his distance so he's out of view as he follows. Eventually the bus stops just outside Andrea's house. She gets off talking and laughing on the phone, oblivious to her impending demise. She noisily makes her way into her house and locks the door. Rob stealthily makes his way to the house. Avoiding the street lights.

He easily jumps over the fence and a little dog starts barking. He grabs it and knocks it out with a heavy punch, and lays the dog gently on the soft ground. He makes sure he wasn't spotted. He silently peeks in the living room window and puts her parents to sleep with heavy tranquilizers from his rifle.

Rob easily makes his way to the back door, and very quickly picks the lock and enters. He keeps low, to remain out of sight and makes his way upstairs to find Andrea. He hears her in the toilet and darts into her room. He hides behind the door just as she enters. He slowly shuts the door and locks it. He flicks the light on and Andrea jumps as she sees him in her bedside table mirror. She turns slowly round to face him, frozen in fear.

Andrea Smith

(Shaken)

Who... are you? What do... you want from me?

Robert Sanders

(Voice Distorted)

I'm simply the messenger, you conniving little slut...

Rob pulls out a dessert eagle gun with a silencer attached and shoots her in the leg. She instantly falls the carpeted floor as Rob begins to tower over her. She looks at him in a pleading way. But he ignores it as he again fires another round, and it hits her in the stomach. And she winces in severe pain. Her life slowly ebbs away as blood slowly pools around her.

Andrea Smith

(Pleading)

Please... don't kill me. Why... are you doing this?

Robert Sanders

Payback bitch!

He aims and simply shoots her in the head. More of her blood spurts everywhere and her body instantly goes limp. Robert hides his gun and quickly sneaks back out the house. We hear the whistle coming from his bike getting fainter as rides away.

It is the next day and Rob is in normal clothes, jeans and a white t-shirt. He is walking through town. By sheer coincidence he spots his next target which is Lucy. He quickly follows her as he enters a nearby ladies shop. He stalks her as she grabs dresses and heads to the changing rooms. Luckily for Rob there not curtains. They lock from the inside, and there big enough for two people. He quickly nips in in front of her.

He quickly puts on a black balaclava conveniently concealed in his packet pocket, as well as leather gloves. He forcibly grabs her, locks the door and covers her mouth.

Robert Sanders

(Gruffly)

Don't make a fucking sound bitch!

Lucy Evans

(Muffled)

Please....

Robert Sanders

You knew this was coming you fucking lying slut Any final words?

Lucy Evans

I'm... sorry.

He quickly jerks her neck and a violent bone breaking snap is heard as her body instantly goes limp. He sits her on the bench in the dressing room and puts her in a convincing sleeping position, and closes her eyes. He peaks out the door to make sure he won't be spotted as he takes off the gloves and balaclava. He darts quickly out the shop and into the crowd outside. Quickly making himself indistinguishable from them.

Part 6: Convincing Lies

few months have passed since Rob killed Lucy and Andrea. He is inside an interrogation room at the local police station. He is sitting in the chair opposite, arms folded and expressionless. The door opens and two men in smart clothes enter. Rob just glances at them disinterested. They close the door and sit down and one of them slaps a folder on the table. Rob doesn't even react.

Man One

I'm Chief Inspector Johnson, this is my colleague chief inspector Ford.

Robert Sanders

Ok...

Chief Inspector Ford

We know you killed miss Evans and miss Smith.

Chief Inspector Johnson

What my.... colleague is trying to say is, we're currently investigating the deaths of...

Robert Sanders

And you think I did it?

Chief Inspector Ford

Don't play dumb! We know you did. I've read your file... Dead Eye!

Robert Sanders

(Eerily Calm)

Don't you fucking dare call me that. I'm no longer that person anymore.

Chief Inspector Johnson

The wounds on Andrea's body, do tell us they came from your old rifle. Which you named "Night Stalker"

Chief Inspector Ford

I agree.

Robert Sanders

Are you certain of that? Can you back up these allegations. My rifle is, locked up and stored correctly in the proper manner.

Chief Inspector Ford

(Angrily)

Cut the shit rob, you know you did it. We know you did it, so fucking tell us the truth and stop bullshitting.

A officer quickly enters and passes over a piece of paper and Ford snatches it and the officer quickly leaves and closes the door as Ford reads it.

Chief Inspector Ford

(Pissed)

Fuck!

Chief Inspector Johnson

What is it!

Chief Inspector Ford

The results came back. The wounds and ammunition used, don't match. There... inconclusive... your... free to go... Mr Sanders.

Rob stands up and begins to leave but Ford grabs him and Rob just stares right through him. Ford quickly regains his composure.

Chief Inspector Ford

(Through clenched teeth)

I fucking know you did this, you lying piece of shit. I'll find the evidence... when I do, I'll nail you to the fucking wall.

Rob grips ford's hand with force, squeezing it until it nearly brakes and shoves it away ad Ford reflexively shakes off the pain. Rob smiles eerily at him, which makes him uncomfortable. He carries on as we follow him out. He sees Chloe waiting on him, leaning on her car. They both smile reassuringly at each other. They hug and kiss each other passionately.

Chloe Davidson

What they say babe?

Robert Sanders

Not much, tried to pin shit on me. Nothing usual.

Chloe Davidson

Were you... careful baby?

Robert Sanders

Naturally.

Chloe Davidson

What about there parents babe?

Robert Sanders

They'll grieve, but there innocent in all this. The... little packages they had, a little more than they realised.

From nowhere Kirsty storms up to Rob crying. She grabs him and screams in his face.

Kirsty Watson

THERE FUCKING DEAD BECAUSE OF YOU...

Robert Sanders

(Calmly)

Careful Kirsty. Telling lies, can get a person in **SERIOUS** trouble. Now calm the fuck down.

Kirsty Watson

Why Rob? Just why?

Robert Sanders

I don't know what your talking about!

Chloe Davidson

Me neither babe.

Kirsty Watson

You dumb fuck, I know you did it.

Rob grabs her by the arm and leads her to Chloe's car, he slams her hard against and looks her dead in the eyes.

Robert Sanders

(Whispering)

Listen here, you little shit. If you want me to kill you, here and now. I can easily do that and make it look like a suicide. Remember bitch, I'm a trained killer. I can end you in so many ways. Now... keep... your... fucking trap shut.

Kirsty Watson

(Pleading)

Please Rob, stop this. I beg you... we can talk about this.... like adults.

Robert Sanders

You can't fucking talk your way out this time, Kirsty... You've crossed the line... you'll never know when I'm coming for you... I'll see you **VERY** soon.

He forcibly lets her go. She stares into his eyes, knowing his training has kicked in. Chloe nods to her to leave. She runs off and into one of her thug cousins. She nods to him to look at Rob, who in turn gives them the thousand yard stare. They quickly cross the street to avoid them. Without warning a military vehicle passes them, which parks up after seeing Rob. Its his c.o. he walks up to Rob who instantly salutes him. Chloe smiles genuinely. He smiles back.

C.O. Henderson

Lieutenant Sanders! How are you?

Robert Sanders

Fine sir... just fine.

C.O. Henderson

You've got that look in your eye, Sanders.

Robert Sanders

Sir?

C.O. Henderson

Dead Eye... I know it's you.

Robert Sanders

(Gruffly)

Commander!

Chloe Davidson

Baby? You... alright?

C.O. Henderson

No, he's not I'm afraid. To deal with the carnage of war, his mind developed a... alter ego. It named itself dead Eye. It... I mean he took over, when the situation was too overwhelming and dangerous. I can only assume... something has occurred.

Chloe Davidson

(Whispering)

He's um... taken care of some people who planned for people to beat him up.

C.O. Henderson

Oh no! Dead Eye? Where's Robert!

Dead Eye

Safe! I'm doing what he can't sir. You know this.

Chloe Davidson

Your... not my Robbie.

Dead Eye

No shit lady... simple really, they beat him up... I came out.

C.O. Henderson

Dead Eye, I'm ordering you to stand down.

Chloe Davidson

Please!

Dead Eye

Negative sir, sorry lady I can't. Don't get involved... for Roberts sake...

C.O. Henderson

Miss Davidson, please accompany me to headquarters. This will only escalate.

Dead Eye

He's right lady, best keep out of this. We don't want you hurt.

Chloe Davidson

I love you baby.

Dead Eye

He... loves you too.

Dead Eye salutes them both, as they walk to the military vehicle, and watches as they drive off. Robert briefly comes through. His voice is more gentle than the other personality.

Robert Sanders

I know you have to do this.

Dead Eye

I know kid... it didn't have to be this way.

Robert Sanders

You came out, soon as those bastards rushed me.

Dead Eye

No one hurts us. Those are the rules. You play with fire, you get burned.

Robert Sanders

So what's the play here?

Dead Eye

Well her shit scared cousins will give us a wide birth, the cops don't have shit on us... our main target will probably stay in one place. We can't strike while it's light. Darkness is our friend...

Robert Sanders

You do this, then you go back to sleep.

Dead Eye

Yes Robert... I promise...

Robert Sanders.

Ok... Dead Eye... my loyal companion.

Dead Eye

Yes Rob?

Robert Sanders

One word.. End game.

Dead Eye

Yes Sanders. No objections.

Dead Eye takes full control of robs body and quickly moves on.

Final Part: Tying Up Loose Ends...

It's early morning. Kirsty's cousins are hanging around outside a local garage, waiting on there car being serviced. One of them is smoking a cigarette. We see the brief outline of Robert aka Dead Eye, as he sneaks behind them. He grabs the one smoking the cigarette, dragging him behind the nearby skip. He holds him tight in a sleeper hold, drawing his razor sharp knife. Within a blink of an eye he is bleeding profusely from his neck and instantly falls to the ground dead, while blood is pouring into the storm drain.

The other cousin comes out of the garage, looking for his brother.

Bruce Watson

Jake ?... is that you bro? Were did you disappear to?

Dead Eye comes out of the shadows brandishing his blood soaked knife, grinning. Bruce stands there in shock and in fear. He keeps eyeing the knife, then slowly meeting dead eye's gaze.

Dead Eye

Surprised to see me, brucey boy? Oh, your brother won't be bothering us right now, because he's um... dead!

Bruce Watson

You sick fuck... I'll...

Dead Eye

What? Kill me? Ha! I'd like to see you try.

Bruce Watson

Listen bro, we had no choice. We were protecting Kirsty

Dead Eye

Oh, you mean the back stabbing little slut, that's on my naughty list...

Bruce Watson

Hey, that's uncalled for.

Dead Eye

It's the truth, but don't worry your pretty little head... she's next...

Bruce Watson

Look, we only gave you a light beating man. Can't we
move past this?

Dead Eye

Save it.... your done... oh, and don't shout for help!
Or this knife is going straight in your head. So you
can either, attempt to run. Or you walk over here to
me, and I end you quick and painless.

Bruce Watson

Don't have much of a choice, do I!

Dead Eye

That's the spirit brucey boy. Now, be a good little
doggy and come to papa!

Bruce sighs and walks towards dead Eye. Who in turn
salutes him briefly. A few tense moments pass, then
without warning dead eye slits Bruce's throat, he falls
instantly dead to the ground as blood spurts out the
wound. Dead Eye cleans off his knife and casually
whistles as he walks away as Bruce's now lifeless body
stares at him.

Several hours later. We see Kirsty outside her mothers
house. She is on the phone to Rebecca, who informs

her about the fate of her two cousins. She is crying heavily. She hangs up after saying goodbye to Rebecca'. She just stands there with her arms folded, sobbing.

Dead Eye

Poor whittle Kirsty! Cwying for her big cousins. Boohoo.... boo hoo.

Kirsty turns to face dead Eye who is smiling smugly. She just angrily stares at him.

Kirsty Watson

Go to hell Rob....

Dead Eye

Wrong answer, try again bitch!

Kirsty Watson

(Shocked)

Dead... Eye?

Dead Eye

Ding! Right answer, and your prize is.... your dead....

Kirsty Watson

I won't make it easy for you fucker.

Dead Eye

Oh... she's a fighter... but no, your no match for me.
You've got balls ill give you that... Shall we dance?

Kirsty tries to run back into her mothers house, but dead eye anticipates this move and throws his knife with acute accuracy. It hits kirsty straight in the back and falls instantly, trying not to yell out in pain. She tries to crawl back inside. But any exertion drains her energy quickly. She crawls backwards towards the fence and uneasily sits up, quickly glancing up at the living room window. She smiles smugly, as dead Eye confidently walks towards her. He leans down to mock her.

Dead Eye

Any final thoughts, bitch?

Kirsty Watson

(Laboured Breathing)

Just one... see... you... in... hell.. you... dumb bitch....

She smiles one last time as she gestures to look at the window, as she slumps dead. He turns to see Kirsty's mum on the phone to the police. He slowly stands, reeling in shock. Dead Eye knows she's innocent and can't kill her. He just walks out the gate and soberly sits on the ground. We hear sirens in the distance getting closer. From nowhere police cars and a few vans surround him. Dead Eye drops the knife and gives up. He slowly raises his hands up to show he's unarmed.

Robert Sanders

Well old friend, this is it.... no smooth talking out of this shit show.

Dead Eye

No argument there Bobby boy!

Robert Sanders

We had a... Good run!

Dead Eye

(Chuckles)

Yeah, but it's done now...

Robert Sanders

Straight to jail... do not pass go!

Dead Eye

Yup, I'll try and....

Robert Sanders

It's ok, you've taught me how to survive.

Dead Eye

I'll always watch your back, if you need me....

Robert Sanders

I know bud.... I know....

We slowly drift backwards to see officers cautiously approach him. Robert places his hands behind his back as he is cuffed. He looks to find Chloe, but knows she wouldn't want to see him like this. Chief Inspector Johnson, takes over to lead Rob away, who smiles genuinely at him, who in turn smiles back, knowing Rob is back in control

Robert Sanders

Inspector.... I'm....

Chief Inspector Johnson

(Softly)

I know Rob... I know....

We watch as Rob is lead away into an awaiting police car. The other officers get back in there vehicles and they all drive off. The streets become eerily quiet again as we hear the sirens fade into the distance...

Fin....?